P9-BZS-247

$ .75 +TX

DOG'S
COLORFUL DAY

Copyright © 2000 by Tucker Slingsby Ltd
All rights reserved.
Devised and produced by Tucker Slingsby Ltd
Roebuck House, 288 Upper Richmond Road West, London SW14 7JG.
Design by Helen James

CIP Data is available.

Published in the United States 2001 by Dutton Children's Books,
a division of Penguin Young Readers Group
345 Hudson Street, New York, New York 10014
www.penguin.com
Typography by Richard Amari
Printed in Singapore • First American Edition
ISBN 0-525-46528-6
4 6 8 10 9 7 5 3

DOG'S
COLORFUL DAY

A Messy Story about Colors and Counting
Emma Dodd

Dutton Children's Books
New York

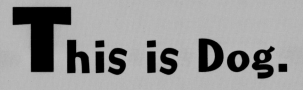
This is Dog.

As you can see,
Dog is white with
one black spot on
his left ear.

At breakfast time,
Dog sits under
the table, as usual.

Splat!

A drip of red jam
lands on his back.

Now Dog has
two spots.

After breakfast, Dog runs outside.

He slips past the man
painting the front door.

Splish!

His tail dips into
the blue paint.

Now Dog has three spots.

Dog runs to the park
and rolls on the grass.

Squash!

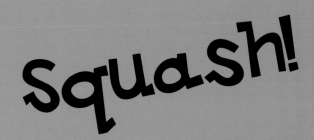

The grass makes a green
stain on his white coat.

Now Dog has four spots.

Dog follows a little boy
eating chocolate.

Squish!

The boy gives Dog a
chocolaty pat—
but no chocolate.

Now Dog has
five spots.

A bee buzzes up to see what is going on.

Swish!

The bee drops yellow pollen as it flies by.

Now Dog has six spots.

Dog trots on
through the park.

Splosh!

A drop of pink
ice cream lands
on his right ear.

Now Dog has
seven spots.

Time to go home.
Dog runs up the street.

A bouncing ball splatters
Dog with gray mud.

Now Dog has eight spots.

In front of the gate,
Dog steps on a carton
of orange juice.

Splurt!

A patch of orange
appears on his leg.

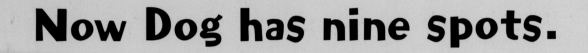

Now Dog has nine spots.

Dog races back inside the house and knocks right into Vicky.

"Silly Dog!"

Vicky's purple marker leaves a smudge on Dog's head.

Now Dog has
ten spots.

**Vicky looks down at Dog.
She counts his colorful spots.**

1   2   3   4   5

6   7   8   9   IO!

Vicky looks more closely.
Dog has . . .

a red spot
of jam,

a blue blob
of paint,

a green stain
of grass,

a yellow
patch
of pollen,

a brown
smear of
chocolate,

a pink **drop** of ice cream,

a gray **splatter** of mud,

an orange **splash** of juice,

a purple **smudge** of ink,

and, of course, a black **spot** on his left ear!

"You need a bath, Dog!"

When Dog climbs into bed,
he has just one black spot
on his left ear.

Good night, Dog.

What a colorful day you've had!